Franklin Goes to the Hospital

With special thanks to the Community Memorial Hospital in Port Perry and The Hospital for Sick Children in Toronto – B.C.

Franklin

Franklin is a trade mark of Kids Can Press Ltd.

Text copyright © 2000 by P.B. Creations Inc.
Illustrations copyright © 2000 by Brenda Clark Illustrator Inc.

Story written by Sharon Jennings.

Interior illustrations prepared with the assistance of Shelley Southern.

Kids Can Press acknowledges the support of the Ontario Arts Council, the Canada Council for the Arts and the Government of Canada, through the BPIDP, for our publishing activity. Canada

Kids Can Press Ltd.
29 Birch Avenue
Toronto, Ontario, Canada
M4V 1E2

Printed in Hong Kong by Wing King Tong Co. Ltd.

CM 00 0 9 8 7 6 5 4 3 2 1
CDN PA 00 0 9 8 7 6 5 4 3 2 1

Canadian Cataloguing in Publication Data

Franklin goes to the hospital

Based on characters created by Paulette Bourgeois and Brenda Clark.

ISBN 1-55074-732-0 (bound)   ISBN 1-55074-734-7 (pbk.)

I. Bourgeois, Paulette.   II. Clark, Brenda.

PS8550.F724 2000   jC813'.54   C99-931786-5
PZ7.F724 2000

Kids Can Press is a Nelvana company

Franklin Goes to the Hospital

Story based on characters created by
Paulette Bourgeois and Brenda Clark
Illustrated by Brenda Clark

Kids Can Press

FRANKLIN sometimes had colds and tummy aches, and every now and then he got cuts and bruises. He went to the doctor's for regular checkups, and once the doctor came to Franklin's house. But, until now, Franklin had never been to the hospital.

Franklin and his friends were playing soccer. The ball was kicked to Franklin, and it hit him hard in the chest.

"Ooof!" he groaned. But he kept on playing.

That night at bathtime Franklin said "Ouch!" when he dried his tummy.

His mother took a closer look.

"Hmmm," she said. "We'll go to the doctor first thing tomorrow."

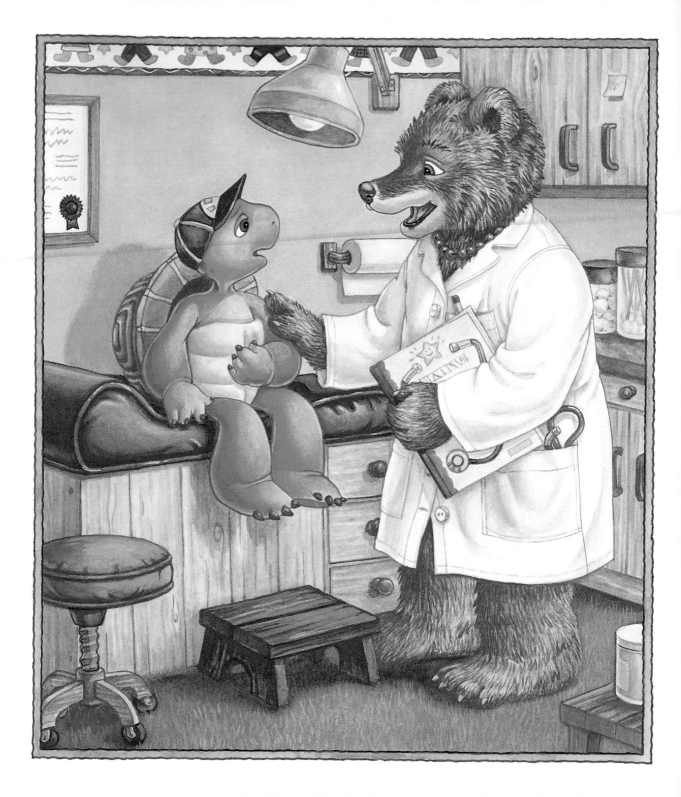

With gentle fingers, Dr. Bear poked and prodded Franklin's shell. She discovered a small crack.

"It isn't serious, Franklin," she said. "But I have to put a pin in your shell to help it grow properly. I'll schedule an operation for you tomorrow morning at the hospital."

"Will it hurt?" asked Franklin.

"We'll give you sleep medicine before the operation, so you won't feel a thing," replied Dr. Bear. "When you wake up, you'll be a little sore. But we'll keep you in the hospital overnight to make sure that you're okay."

Dr. Bear explained that operations can only be done when a patient has an empty stomach. She told Franklin not to eat or drink after bedtime that night.

Franklin didn't mind. His tummy was too busy flip-flopping for him to think about eating.

After school, Franklin's friends came to visit. Franklin showed them the book about hospitals that Dr. Bear had given him. Fox pointed to a picture and asked why everyone was wearing a mask.

"Masks keep germs out of the operating room," explained Franklin.

"Are you scared?" asked Beaver.

"Of course he's not scared," replied Bear. "Franklin's very brave."

Franklin didn't say anything.

It was early when Franklin and his parents left for the hospital. With his blue blanket and Sam clutched in his arms, Franklin said goodbye to his room.

Franklin's mother gave him a hug. "You'll be home tomorrow," she reminded him.

"I know," Franklin said softly.

"You're a very brave little turtle," said his father.

At the hospital, Franklin was given a bracelet with his name on it. Then an attendant pushed him down a long hallway in a wheelchair.

Franklin stared at all the strange equipment on carts and trolleys, and he wrinkled his nose at the unfamiliar smells. As they went around corners and through doors, Franklin kept checking to make sure that his parents were keeping up.

At last, they reached Franklin's room.

A nurse gave Franklin a special gown to wear. She took his temperature and his blood pressure and listened to his heart. Next she rubbed some cream on his hand.

"This will numb your hand," she told him. "Then it won't hurt when the doctor puts in the needle for your sleep medicine."

"Okay," said Franklin in a small voice.

"You're a very brave patient," said the nurse.

Soon the attendant came back to take Franklin to another room. Dr. Bear was waiting for him.

"We're going to take some X-rays," she said. "I need to know exactly where to put the pin."

"I don't want X-rays," whispered Franklin.

"X-rays don't hurt," explained Dr. Bear. "The machine only takes pictures of what's inside you."

"I know," said Franklin.

He started to cry.

Dr. Bear sat down beside Franklin.

"Please tell me what's wrong," she said.

Franklin sniffled. "Everybody thinks I'm brave, but I've just been pretending. X-rays will show that *inside* I'm scared."

"Oh Franklin!" exclaimed Dr. Bear. "An X-ray doesn't show feelings. It only shows shell and bones."

"You mean no one will know I'm afraid?" Franklin asked.

"No one," replied Dr. Bear. "But just because you're afraid doesn't mean you aren't brave. Being brave means doing what you have to do, no matter how scared you feel."

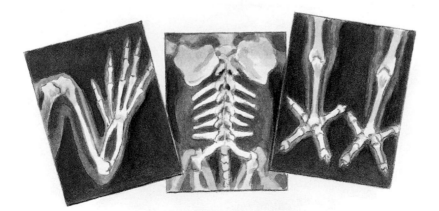

Franklin thought for a few moments.
"Well, I am scared to have the operation,"
he finally said. "But I know I have to so my shell
will grow big and strong."

Dr. Bear smiled. "That's what being brave is all about."

Franklin let out a very deep sigh.

"I'm ready now," he said.

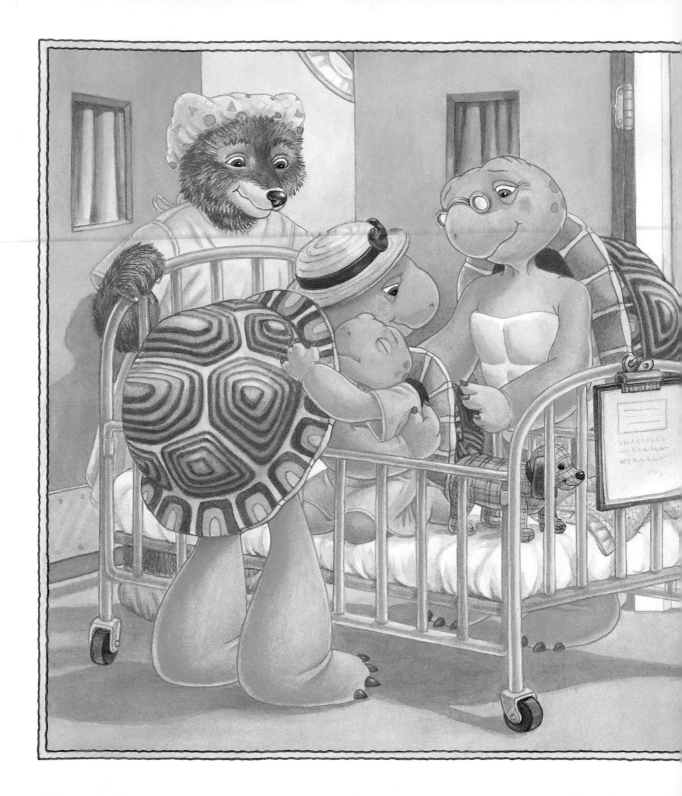

When the X-rays were done, Franklin was taken to the waiting room.

"We aren't allowed into the operating room, Franklin," said his father.

"But we'll be with you in the recovery room when you wake up," his mother promised.

Soon Dr. Bear came to get Franklin. His mother and father kissed him and waved as he went through the doors.

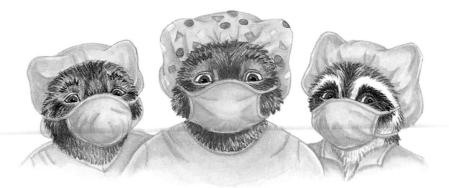

In the operating room, Franklin said hello to the other doctors and nurses. Dr. Bear put stickers on Franklin's chest and explained that this was how they would watch his breathing and heartbeat during the operation.

Then Dr. Raccoon put the needle for the sleep medicine in Franklin's hand. It didn't hurt at all. When that was done, he asked Franklin to count backwards from one hundred.

"But I can only count backwards from ten," Franklin said.

"That will be just fine," said Dr. Bear.

"Ten, nine, eight ..." began Franklin.

And that was as far as he got.

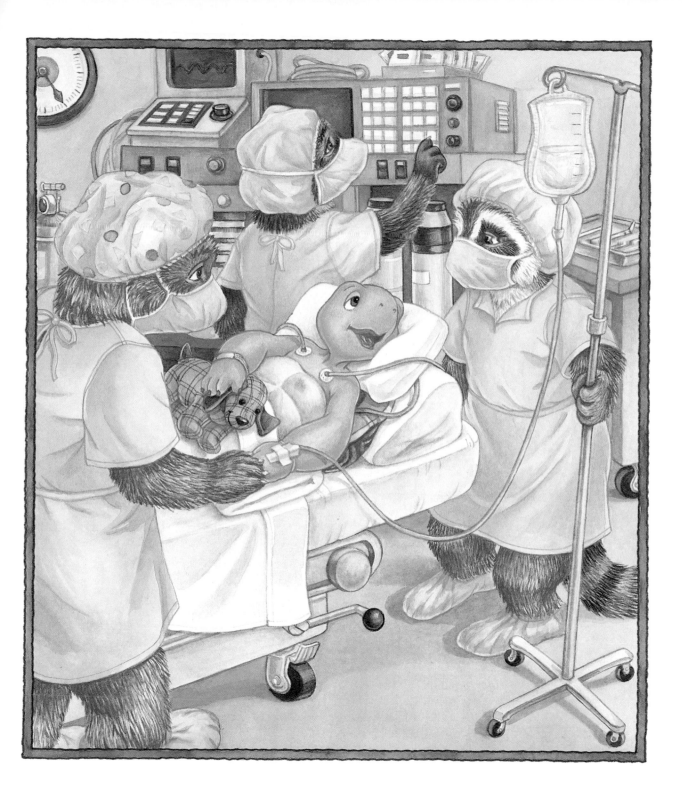

"Wake up, Franklin," called a faraway voice.

But Franklin didn't want to wake up. In his dream he was scoring the winning goal.

"Wake up now, Franklin," said his mother.

Slowly, Franklin opened his eyes. He saw his parents and Dr. Bear, and then he remembered.

"I haven't finished counting," he said in a wobbly voice.

"But I've finished operating," said Dr. Bear with a laugh.

Two hours later, Franklin was back in his hospital room. He walked slowly to the mirror and looked at his bandages.

"I guess it'll be a while before I can play soccer again," he sighed.

"Dr. Bear thinks you'll heal very quickly," said Franklin's father.

"She also said you're an excellent patient," added his mother.

Franklin smiled.

That night, after Franklin's parents had gone home, Dr. Bear came to see him.

"I have something to show you, Franklin," she said. She held up an X-ray.

"Is that me?" he asked.

Dr. Bear nodded. "That's you," she said. "Brave through and through."